D1451247

Authors Page

Pat Goldys is a retired principal who started writing children's books during the pandemic of 2020. She enjoys writing books that teach a lesson. She is co-authoring with Marlene Everhardt, who is a CODA, child of deaf adult, on a series of books about grandma, who is deaf and her grandchildren's discovery and learning of sign language. As the past principal at Villa Cresta Elementary, a school with an integrated program for the deaf and hard of hearing, she learned sign language and developed lasting relationships with some of these amazing students.

Marlene Shipley Everhardt lives in Harford County, Maryland with her husband and family. She worked for many years in the private sector and is thrilled to have co-authored her first children's book with her high school friend of fifty years, Pat Goldys. Having grown up a CODA (hearing child of deaf adults) with ASL being her first language, she is happy to share her love of the deaf language and culture through "Grandma's Ears Are Broken" and continue her legacy. When she is not co-authoring with Pat, you can find her at the beach flying her kite or enjoying tea time with her wonderful girlfriends!

Gratitude

Special Thanks

Our heartfelt thanks to Erin R., Mary H. and Becki L., our "tell us what you think" book review crew. Your honest comments and encouragement for our project are warmly appreciated.

Dedication

A sweet remembrance to my deaf parents, Evelyn and Edward Shipley, who raised me to see that even though what some may lack in one sense - we are given tenfold with our other senses. They showed me love, and taught me respectfulness and acceptance. This is dedicated to the both of you.
-Marlene

To Ray and Theresa Helinski, the best parents anyone could ever want. They taught me to appreciate differences in all people and value others' friendships and talents.I had a wonderful life growing up with such remarkable parents!
-Pat

Alex is a happy boy who likes to talk a lot.

He has a lot to say for such a little tot.

He loves his Grandma and visits frequently.

She always listens and smiles consistently!

GIRL   BOY   TALK

One day Grandma was cooking something to eat.

Alex was chatting and Grandma did not speak.

He repeated his question, no words still!

"I am thirsty. Can I have a milk refill?"

MILK

THIRSTY

Alex tapped Grandma's back with his hand.

"Can you hear me? I don't understand."

Grandma turned around and smiled ear to ear.

Alex said, "Grandma, I was talking. Didn't you hear?"

SMILE

Alex was perplexed. What will happen next?

Alex was worried indeed.

So excitedly he screamed.

WORRIED

"Grandma's ears are broken! I want them fixed for you!"

Grandma looked at Alex and knew what she had to do.

"I am deaf. I can't hear. My ears are quite fine.

I will teach you the wonderful language of sign."

 DEAF

TO TEACH

  BROKEN

Sign will be our way to talk and hear.

We will use our hands and fingers to make our words clear.

It is fun to learn and we will practice,

Until you really know how to do this!

 FUN

People talk in many different ways.

Do you want to learn sign language today?

Then we can SEE our chat with each other.

Sign is another way to communicate that you will discover!

TO LEARN

TO SEE

Alex was excited, nodded yes
To Grandma's language done with finesse.
He was so hungry, his stomach growled,
Grandma pointed to a bowl with a towel.

BOWL

Grandma says with voice and sign,
"If you are hungry, then we shall eat.
We will make pizza, my favorite treat!

PIZZA   FAVORITE

First we roll the floured dough,

Add the sauce tomato,

Sprinkle cheese, then we take

Pizza to the oven to bake."

Alex waited for what seemed forever,

When will pizza be done, maybe never!

Grandma signed, "Pizza is ready!"

"I know that sign," proudly said he!

BAKE

She put a slice of pizza on a plate,

Handed to Alex which he quickly ate.

Alex thought this pizza delicious,

Grandma smiled..

Pizza is quite nutritious.

PIZZA!

CHEESE

Grandma exclaims,

"We learned some signs to communicate!

Let's do something fun to celebrate!

There is a special pizzeria design,

Where customers and staff sign and dine!

CELEBRATE    PLATE

This pizzeria is run by only the deaf.

Servers, cashier, manager and chef!

We will order our food with gestures of sign.

The staff will sign back each and every time!"

COOK

ORDER

Alex and Grandma love to talk in sign everyday!

They move their hands in ways to convey,

The words they "show" instead of say.

Do you want to learn sign language today?

LOVE

Made in the USA
Columbia, SC
05 March 2021